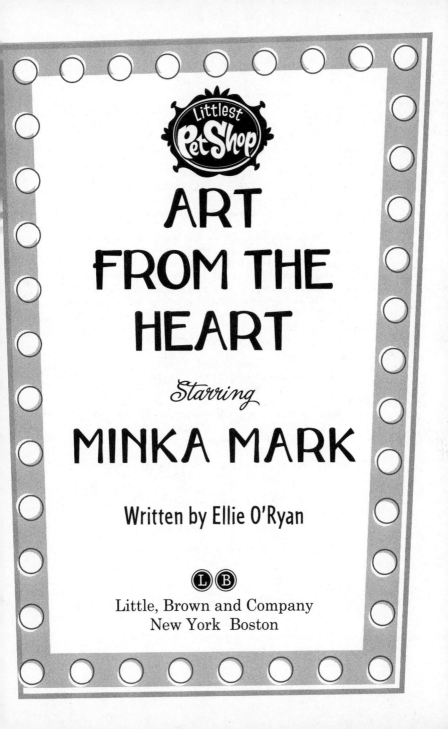

Littlest Pet Shop

ART FROM THE HEART

Starring

MINKA MARK

Written by Ellie O'Ryan

Ⓛ Ⓑ

Little, Brown and Company
New York Boston

Little, Brown and Company

Hachette Book Group
1290 Avenue of the Americas, New York, NY 10104
Visit us at lb-kids.com

Little, Brown and Company is a division of Hachette Book Group, Inc. The Little, Brown name and logo are trademarks of Hachette Book Group, Inc.

The publisher is not responsible for websites (or their content) that are not owned by the publisher.

First Edition: January 2016

ISBN 978-0-316-30154-1

10 9 8 7 6 5 4 3 2 1

RRD-C

Printed in the United States of America

To Megan Ruggiero,
who puts heart in all she does

CONTENTS

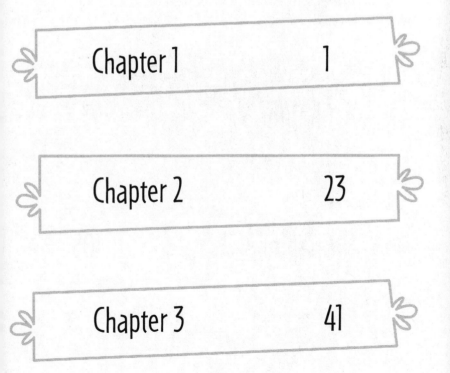

Chapter 1	1
Chapter 2	23
Chapter 3	41

Chapter 4	59
Chapter 5	77
Chapter 6	93
Chapter 7	105

Chapter 8   125

Chapter 9   135

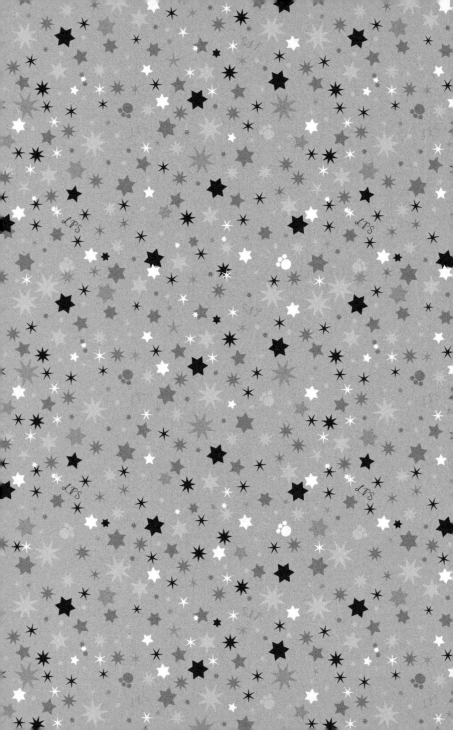

Chapter 1

Minka Mark burst into the Littlest Pet Shop, chattering with excitement as her owner dropped her off. The monkey stood in the middle of the store and shook wildly, sending droplets of water scattering throughout the room. That was a trick Minka had learned from one of her best pet pals, Zoe, a Cavalier King Charles spaniel. Despite her custom-made Blythe Style rain gear, Minka had still gotten pretty wet on the walk over to Day Camp. And no wonder—it was pouring outside!

Mrs. Twombly, the owner of the Littlest Pet Shop, wasn't upset about the puddles in her store. Instead, she chuckled as she grabbed a rag from under the counter. "Go right on back, Minka," she said as she began to mop up the mess. "Everybody else is here already. I know they'll be happy to see you!"

Still chattering, Minka catapulted through the curtain that separated Day Camp from the rest of the store and skidded to a sudden stop. Something was wrong—very wrong. Sure, it was dark and stormy outside...but why did her friends' faces look so dark and stormy, too? On an ordinary day, everybody else was just as excited about spending time at Day Camp as Minka.

So what was the problem?

Minka tilted her head as she studied the room. Fashion fanatic Zoe was organizing her nail polish with a dejected look on her face. Each colorful bottle went *clink* as she dropped it into a plastic case.

Russell the hedgehog was normally a bustling bundle of energy, full of plans and tasks that needed to be accomplished. But when Zoe spied him, he was staring out the window, absentmindedly tallying the bolts of lightning that flashed through the sky.

Penny Ling, the gentle and innocent panda, was muttering to herself as she attempted to thread a needle. A torn ribbon stick on the floor beside her told Minka all she needed to know about why Penny Ling was in a grumpy mood.

Even Pepper the skunk, who was so funny she could turn just about anything into a great joke, looked glum as she sprawled across a plush pet bed and stared at the ceiling.

Well, this *is no good,* Minka thought. *Where are Vinnie and Sunil? They'll know how to brighten things up around here.*

Minka found Vinnie the gecko and Sunil the mongoose in front of the TV. That was no surprise—Vinnie and Sunil were best friends after all. They were practically inseparable, but instead of settling in to watch TV together, Vinnie and Sunil were battling over the remote control. They yanked it back and forth, back and forth, like they were playing tug-of-war. Minka could see with one glance that this definitely wasn't a game.

"It's my turn to choose the show!" hollered Sunil.

"No, it's *my* turn!" Vinnie shot back.

Uh-oh, Minka thought as Vinnie and Sunil shouted at each other. *This isn't going to end well.*

Just then—*sproing!*

The back of the remote flew off, and four small batteries zinged through the air.

Crack! One of the batteries knocked a bottle of nail polish from Zoe's paw, causing her to spill it all over herself.

"No!" Zoe howled as nail polish dripped all over the floor. "Ravenous Red is my *favorite!*"

Zip! Another battery knocked the needle right out of Penny Ling's paw.

"Oh, come on!" the panda moaned. "I *almost* had the needle threaded!"

Bonk! The third battery bounced off Russell's head.

"Ow!" yelped the hedgehog as he rubbed his forehead, being careful not to touch any of his prickly quills.

Zoom! The fourth and final battery flew straight at Minka—but with a quick side step, she was able to grab it. "Yes!" Minka cheered. Before anyone could congratulate her on her speedy reflexes—

Zzzap! At that moment, the lights flickered twice, then went out. Even the TV was dark and silent. There was no doubt about it: The storm had knocked out the power, leaving seven pets in a dark room with nothing to do.

Everybody groaned at once—everybody except Minka.

"So much for fixing my ribbon stick," Penny Ling said with a sigh.

"Now I can't even tell my Peach Pie polish from my Orange Sherbet polish," Zoe complained.

"I can't believe I'm going to miss my show," Sunil moaned as he flopped onto a cushy beanbag chair.

"And *I* can't believe *I'm* going to miss *my* show!" Vinnie groaned.

Before they could start fighting again, Mrs. Twombly poked her head through the curtain. "Goodness, that's a big storm out there!" she cried. "But don't worry, everybody. I'm sure the power will be back on in no time. And even better, Blythe will be here soon!"

Finally, some good news, Minka thought. All the pets adored Blythe Baxter, their amazing human friend. Blythe was fun, sweet, loving, and unbelievably creative—and she also had a very special talent. Instead of just hearing barks and growls and squawks and squeaks, Blythe could actually *understand* the animals when they spoke. For Blythe's pet friends, having a human who could truly communicate with them was a wonderful thing. Of course, Blythe had to keep her ability top secret. People just wouldn't be able to believe that all those cute little animal noises were actually words—or that animals could understand every single thing that was said around them.

Minka turned to face her friends. "What's going on, you guys?" she asked. "I haven't seen everybody in such bad moods since the tasty-treat truck crashed and spilled an entire year's supply of treats into the river."

Sunil shook his head sadly. "That was a real tragedy," he said as Vinnie pretended to wipe away a tear. "All those treats turned into fish food!"

"Well, sure, I guess, but that's not my point," Minka continued. "Why are we letting a little rain ruin our day?"

"Because, Minka, there's nothing to *do*," replied Zoe. "It's raining too hard to go to the park…"

"And with the power out, it's too dark to read…" added Russell.

"Or sew," Penny Ling spoke up.

"And forget about TV," Sunil and Vinnie said at the same time.

"That doesn't mean we can't have fun!" Minka insisted. "I *promise* we can figure out something great to do today!"

"But how?" Pepper asked. "No TV, no

park, no nail polish, no reading, no ribbon stick—no fun!"

For a moment, Minka was stumped. She'd made a big promise to her friends, and now she needed to deliver. But what could they do in a dark Day Camp while a tremendous thunderstorm raged outside?

Suddenly, inspiration struck.

"Glow tag!" Minka shrieked. In the dim light, she couldn't see her friends' faces very well, but she thought they seemed interested. "I have this great glow-in-the-dark paint, and it comes in a whole bunch of colors, so we can each have a color to put on our hands—or, um, paws—"

"Or sticky webbed feet!" Vinnie spoke up.

"Or sticky webbed feet," Minka echoed. "Then we all run around in the dark and try to tag each other. Whoever gets tagged also gets a glowing handprint—I mean, paw print—or footprint—"

"Ooh, that sounds really fun!" exclaimed Pepper.

"But messy," Russell added. Minka didn't need to see his face to know it was all scrunched up in an anxious frown.

"Don't worry about that," Minka reassured him. "We can wear our old T-shirts from the Petwalk Fund-raiser last year and play in the grooming station. After all, it's designed to be hosed down."

"And after this game, I think we'll *all* need to be hosed down," Zoe joked. "Besides, I couldn't possibly get any messier than I already am!" She held up her paws, which were still drenched with a very uneven coat of Ravenous Red polish.

"Everybody, go get your T-shirts!" Minka

announced. "I'll grab my paints. Meet you in the grooming station in ten minutes!"

It wasn't easy to find everything they needed in the dark, but all the pets were so eager to play glow tag that soon everybody was ready for the game.

"Line up over here," Minka told her friends.

"Over where?" asked Vinnie.

"I can't see a thing!" Sunil said.

"Hang on, everybody!" Russell called out. "I've got a flashlight."

Click! Just like that, there was enough light for the pets to see where they needed to stand.

Minka twirled a paintbrush through her fingers like a miniature baton. "Who's first?" she asked.

"I'll go!" Pepper exclaimed.

Minka pranced over to Pepper and painted some neon green paint on her paws while Russell held the flashlight. Pepper giggled. "That tickles!" she said.

"Done!" Minka announced. "Russell, turn off the flashlight for a second, would you?"

"Sure," Russell replied. Suddenly, the grooming station was pitch-black—except for Pepper's glowing paws.

"Whoa! That's awesome!" Pepper said. She waved her paws in the air, leaving glowing green streaks in their wake. "Look at meeeeee!"

The other pets crowded around Minka. In the darkness, she could hear "Me next!" "No, me!" and "Pretty, pretty, pretty, please! Pick me!"

"Russell—flashlight *on!*" Minka yelled. "Don't worry, everybody. I've got enough paint for all of us!"

Working as quickly as she could, Minka painted each pet's paws. Hot pink for Zoe, electric blue for Vinnie, shocking purple for Penny Ling, neon orange for Sunil, and Day-Glo yellow for Russell. The last color, an intense shade of red, Minka used for her own hands. Soon they were ready to play!

"With glow tag, nobody's 'it,'" Minka explained. "The goal is for everybody to tag as many pets as you can. On your mark, get set, *go!*"

Whoosh!

In a flash of neon colors, the pets zoomed off in all directions. Minka followed on their heels, zigging and zagging through the darkness.

"Tag!" Minka shrieked as she touched Pepper's shoulder.

"Oh!" Pepper exclaimed in surprise, spinning around. "I didn't even see you coming!"

"That's the idea!" Minka replied, laughing so hard that she didn't even notice that Russell had crept up behind her until she felt him tap the tip of her tail. Minka tried to whip her long tail away—but it was too late. Now Minka was the only monkey in the whole wide world with a glow-in-the-dark tail!

The tile walls of the grooming station echoed with squeals and laughter as the pets chased each other. Minka was having so much fun that she wished the game would never end. But then, without warning—

Zzzap!

With an unsteady flicker, the lights came

back on. Everybody froze in place. Minka glanced from one friend to another and couldn't help giggling at the sight of the other pets. Everyone was splattered with a rainbow of glow-in-the-dark paint!

"It sure looks like you've been making the best of a stormy situation!" a voice said.

Minka turned around to see Blythe standing in the doorway, a wide grin on her face.

"Blythe!" Minka squealed. "When did you get here?"

"About ten minutes ago," Blythe replied as the pets crowded around her. "I could tell from all the commotion that there was some serious fun going on back here, but— wow! You've outdone yourselves!"

"Don't you mean we *outfunned* ourselves?" Pepper joked, making everyone laugh.

"Glow tag—what an awesome idea," Blythe continued. She tapped her chin thoughtfully. "Hmm...I seem to remember someone getting a set of glow-in-the-dark paint just last week. Minka, was this your idea?"

"Guilty!" Minka said proudly.

"I had a feeling," Blythe said. "That's just one of the things I love about you, Minka. No matter what's going on, you always find a way to make the best of it."

Then Blythe turned to face the whole group.

"I can guess what's next on the agenda," she continued. "Bath time! But first, I have news. *Big* news."

Minka was so intrigued that her tail sprang into a curlicue. From Zoe's perked-up ears to Russell's quivering quills, she could tell that everyone else was just as eager to hear Blythe's announcement.

"Blythe, darling, don't leave us in suspense!" Zoe exclaimed. "Spill it!"

Blythe took a deep breath. "I have received a very exciting invitation," she began.

"A movie premiere?" Zoe cried.

"Uh...no," Blythe told her.

"Are we going to walk the runway at the International Pet Fashion Expo?" asked Zoe.

"Not exactly," replied Blythe. "It's—"

"A gala ball for the Downtown City Museum?" Zoe guessed.

Blythe shook her head. "Not this time," she said. "In fact, it's something even more amazing. I've been invited to design an exclusive line of clothing for the Endangered Animals Fund!"

All the pets broke into happy applause.

Minka clapped louder than anyone, even if she didn't exactly know what Blythe was talking about. After all, Blythe designed new clothes for her very own fashion line, Blythe Style, all the time. What made this one so extra special?

"There are a bunch of reasons why this is such a big deal," Blythe said, as if she could read Minka's mind. "First, it's a joint collection—for pets *and* people. How cool is that? Picture it: You and your owner wearing matching outfits, tailored to make each of you look your very best!"

"That would be just *fabulous*!" cried Zoe.

"And even more important, some of the profits from sales of this collection will go to the Endangered Animals Fund," Blythe said, wide-eyed at the thought. "Can you *imagine*? Just think of all the endangered animals who could be helped if the collection sells well!"

Blythe grew serious all of a sudden. "Of course, the collection has to be really spectacular if we want to earn the most money possible for the Endangered Animals Fund," she told everyone. "It has to be stylish, first and foremost, but it also has to be different. You know, eye-catching, attention-grabbing— like nothing the fashion world has ever seen before."

Zoe pressed her paw against her chest. "Be still my heart!" she gushed. "This is going to be absolutely *epic*! Groundbreaking fashion is my very favorite kind!"

"That's good, because I'm going to need some help," Blythe said. "This might just be one of the biggest opportunities ever . . . and with so much on the line for the

Endangered Animals Fund, I really don't want to blow it."

"Come on, Blythe, you're pretty much the best designer ever!" Minka assured her. "You could never blow it."

Blythe smiled mysteriously. "I guess not... now that I have my secret weapon," she replied.

"What's that?" asked Minka.

"You!" Blythe announced.

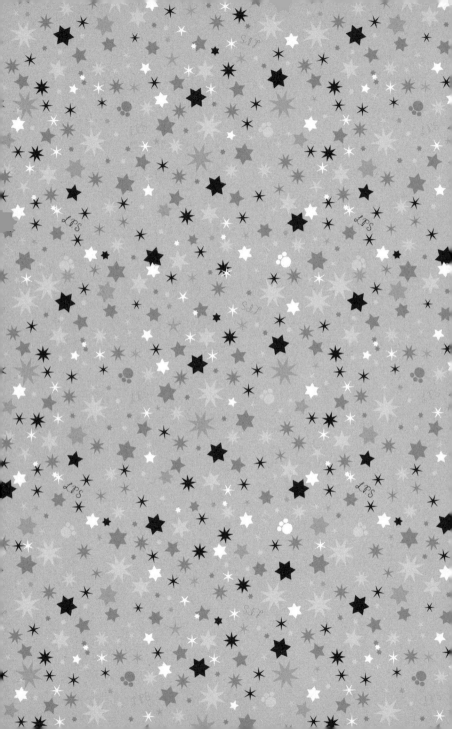

Chapter 2

"Me?" Minka echoed, blinking in surprise. Surely there was a mistake. Like all the pets, Minka was happy to help out whenever Blythe needed an extra model or someone to try on a new design. But what Minka knew about fashion could fit into a thimble. She didn't see how she could possibly be Blythe's secret weapon.

"Yes, you," Blythe said, smiling warmly. "After I got the invitation, I had the most tremendous idea ever: What if the fabrics for this exclusive new line featured animal artwork?"

"Genius," Zoe breathed. "I love it!"

But Minka scrunched up her face in confusion. "Artwork on fabric?" she said. "How would that work? I paint on canvases."

"And T-shirts!" Vinnie said, holding out his paint-splattered shirt.

"And walls and floors, too!" added Sunil as he gestured to the messy grooming station.

"Ha-ha, very funny," Minka said, making a goofy face to show them that she was just teasing. "I wouldn't exactly call that painting. It was more like..."

"Accidental artwork!" Penny Ling suggested.

"Ooh, I like the sound of that!" Minka said. "But I still don't understand how one of my paintings could become an outfit."

"There's this really cool technology," Blythe explained. "You can paint on a canvas, like you always do. Then we'll ship your paintings to a special fabric manufacturer, and they'll make a custom fabric with your painting printed on it."

"Are you serious?" Minka asked in disbelief. "They can do that?"

"They sure can. And just think—if this works out, we could launch the first-ever fashion line designed by pets and people *for* pets and people!" Blythe said excitedly. "What do you say, Minka? Will you do it?"

"Silly Blythe!" Minka exclaimed. "You don't even have to ask. *Of course* I'll do it!"

Blythe clapped her hands together. "Fantastic!" she cried as all the pets cheered.

"But I'm going to need some help," Minka warned her. "I, uh, I really don't know that much about fashion, and knowing the process is part of my method."

"Don't worry about that for even one little second," Zoe assured her. "We'll set up some sort of—oh, I don't know—fashion school for you and teach you everything you need to know."

"You'd do that for me?" Minka asked, bouncing back and forth in excitement.

"Are you kidding? Fashion is my specialty," Zoe replied confidently. "When I'm done, you'll know the difference between satin and sateen…tweed and twill…bias tape and basting…"

"Basting? Like a turkey?" Vinnie asked, licking his lips. "Who knew sewing could be so tasty?"

"Vinnie! It's not the same thing at all!" Blythe said with a smile. "Basting is a way of temporarily holding fabric together, using big, long stitches that can easily be removed. It's helpful when testing out a tricky pattern to make sure that the pieces fit together."

"That's a relief, I guess," joked Pepper. "Otherwise this new fashion line could get pretty *sticky*."

Minka joined in the laughter—but the truth was, she was just as clueless as Vinnie. For the first time, Minka realized just how much she had to learn about fashion.

And she was going to need all the help she could get.

* * *

When Minka arrived at Day Camp the following morning, the weather was still gray and gloomy. Zoe, however, was as bright as a sunbeam as she met Minka and Blythe at the entrance and led them to two chairs.

"Sit. Observe. *Learn*," Zoe ordered.

"Sit? Me? Are you serious?" Minka asked, bouncing excitedly from one arm of the chair to another. "Come on, Zoe! You know sitting's not exactly my strong suit!"

"Well, bounce around as much as you want—as long as you pay attention," Zoe replied. "And get ready for Fast Fashion 101!"

"I know you've seen this before," Blythe began, holding up her sketchbook.

"Sure I have," replied Minka as she whipped out her own identical sketchbook. "I'd be lost without mine."

"So would I!" Blythe agreed. "But while you use yours for drawing all sorts of things, I use mine for fashion designs. See?"

Blythe opened her sketchbook and flipped to a page filled with sketches of adorable pet-sized hats.

"Ahh, last fall's Blythe Style accessories collection," Zoe said in a dreamy voice. "One of my all-time favorites."

"Thanks, Zoe," Blythe said. "So you see, Minka, every article of clothing starts with an idea—and a sketch is the first step to turn that idea into reality."

"Cool!" Minka said. All this time, she'd thought Blythe simply liked drawing outfits and accessories. After all, that was why

Minka loved to paint: for fun. It was definitely her favorite activity.

"Next up—patterns!" Zoe announced as she carefully unfolded several pieces of tissue-thin brown paper.

"This part's really cool," Blythe said. "We use this special paper for all the parts of a particular piece of clothing—like a blouse or a skirt or a coat—and make adjustments until we get just the right fit."

"As you can imagine, a Great Dane needs a much bigger size than a pup like me," Zoe said.

"That's right, Zoe. Pattern pieces can help us figure out different sizes, too," Blythe said, nodding. "Then we use these pieces to cut the fabric before we sew it together."

"The fabric! That's practically my favorite part!" Zoe gushed. "Any color you can imagine, from fluttery silks to stiff brocades. And all of it *gorgeous*!"

"Sunil! Vinnie! You're up!" Blythe called.

There was a long silence while Minka, Blythe, and Zoe waited. At last, Vinnie's voice echoed out from behind a screen. "Do we have to?" he asked.

"Yes, of course you do!" Zoe called back. "Don't you want to help earn money for the Endangered Animals Fund?"

"Well…yeah…" Sunil replied, his voice full of reluctance. "But isn't there an easier way?"

Zoe blinked in amazement. "What could be easier than modeling?" she cried. "Come on, you'll love it!"

"And it will really help Minka to see examples of what we're talking about," Blythe encouraged them.

Minka heard a heavy sigh from behind the screen.

"Oh, *fine*," Vinnie finally said. "Come on, Sunil. Let's get it over with."

When Sunil and Vinnie shuffled out from behind the screen, Minka clapped her hands over her mouth. She didn't *mean* to laugh, exactly. It was just so hard not to! Sunil was wearing a sky-blue silk collared cape, covered in rhinestones and beads, while Vinnie had a purple velvet military cloak with gold tassels on the shoulders.

Sunil looked pained. "It's for a good cause, it's for a good cause, it's for a good cause," he muttered under his breath again and again.

"It absolutely is," Blythe assured him. "Thank you so much—both of you!"

Blythe stood up and spoke to Minka. "I

have to check some things with Mrs. Twombly, so I'm going to turn things over to Zoe now," she said. "Don't worry—you're in good hands—or should I say, *paws.*"

Zoe straightened her shoulders and cleared her throat. "Now, Minka, I know these capes are a little...extreme," she began. "But Blythe whipped them up specially so you could see some fashion in action!"

Zoe launched into a long discussion about the differences between the capes— length and style, cut and trim, seams and darts. Minka tried to pay attention, but soon she was so busy making funny faces with Sunil and Vinnie that she was only half listening to Zoe's lecture—and Zoe was so caught up in what she was saying that she didn't even notice.

At last, Zoe finished, completely worn

out from her big presentation. Sunil and Vinnie seized the opportunity to rip off their capes and scamper back into Day Camp for more fun.

"And *that* is pretty much everything I know about fashion," Zoe said. "*Whew!* That was exhausting."

Minka stifled a yawn. "It sure was," she agreed.

A worried look crossed Zoe's face. "But it was useful, right?" she asked. "I mean, I hope it was."

"Oh, definitely," Minka assured her. "I learned a ton about fashion." *At least, I learned a ton before I tuned out,* Minka thought with a twinge of guilt.

It was the right thing to say, though; Zoe's anxious expression immediately relaxed.

"Thank goodness!" she said. "Because this new line is a *very* big deal. I heard Blythe telling Mrs. Twombly that if we can pull it off—well, there's no saying how much money we might raise for endangered animals. To care for them...protect them... even *save* them, maybe."

Minka gulped. *I didn't think of it quite like that*, she thought, feeling even more guilty for goofing off during the fashion lesson.

"And it all starts with *you!*" Zoe continued brightly. "So I just want you to know, Minka...if there's anything you need, *anything* at all—please, please don't hesitate to ask me. I have a feeling that you're going to create something absolutely *amazing.* Brilliant, even! And I want to help however I can!"

"Well, uh, I'll do my best," Minka replied. "Actually, I'd better get to work right now. There's no time like the present, right?"

"Exactly!" cried Zoe. "Good luck, Minka! You can do it!"

But Minka had already disappeared into Day Camp. "Sketchbook...graphite...colored pencils..." she muttered to herself as she looked for her art supplies. There was just one problem.

Minka's art supplies were nowhere to be found.

Not on the table, not under the hammock, not in Minka's cubby, not in *anybody's* cubby, actually; Minka searched high and low, practically turning Day Camp inside out. She didn't find as much as a stubby crayon or smudgy eraser.

Something very unusual happened then:

A confused frown crossed Minka's face. *I'm not the neatest pet here,* she thought, *but how in the world did I manage to lose* all *my art supplies in just one day?*

That's when Minka realized something else: Where *was* everybody? She was alone in Day Camp—and that was weirder than anything else that had happened so far.

"Blythe?" Minka called. "Sunil? Vinnie? Where did you guys go?"

Click.

It was only the sound of a light switch being flipped on, but it was enough to make Minka jump three feet into the air. Someone was in Blythe's sewing room, and whoever it was must've just turned on the light. Minka could tell from the warm yellow glow that spilled out from behind the door, which was open just a crack.

Blythe will know where everybody is, Minka thought as she scampered toward Blythe's sewing room. *Maybe she'll even know where all my art stuff is, too!*

Minka was so excited to see Blythe that she didn't just knock on the door—she nearly knocked it down. It swung open with a loud *bang*—that's when Minka got the shock of her life!

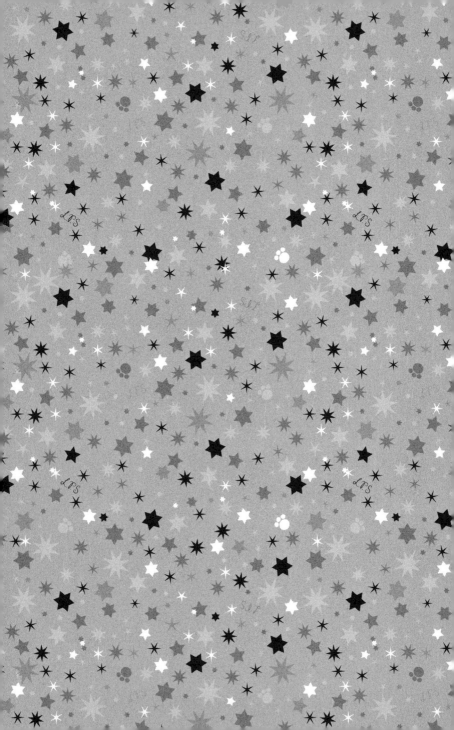

Chapter 3

"Surprise!" a chorus of voices yelled. With wide eyes, Minka glanced around and saw Blythe and Zoe, Sunil and Vinnie, Pepper and Russell and Penny Ling all crowded together in Blythe's sewing room—or, what *used* to be Blythe's sewing room. The small space, normally filled with sewing supplies, had been completely transformed!

On the shelves where Blythe usually kept bolts of fabric, Minka saw several blank canvases in various sizes, all stacked in neat piles. Instead of Blythe's sewing machine on a long table, Minka spotted her own easel, which had been moved from the main room. In the drawers where Blythe always stashed needles, thimbles, pattern pieces, scissors, and spools of thread in every color, Minka saw tons of art supplies: all kinds of paints, from watercolor to oil, sticks of graphite, colored pencils, heavy duty erasers, and more.

What's going on? Minka wondered, puzzled. *How is Blythe going to design an amazing new collection without any of her sewing stuff?*

She glanced back at the enormous grins on her friends' faces, and something clicked.

This isn't a sewing studio anymore, Minka realized. *It's an art studio! And if it's an art studio…*

"You did this for *me*?" Minka was so excited that her voice came out all squeaky and high-pitched, making everyone giggle. "Seriously? For *me*?"

"Why, of course we did!" Zoe replied. "We came up with the big plan yesterday. With such an enormous and important task ahead of you, we figured the *least* we could do is make sure you'd have everything you need!"

"And a real artist's workspace, too," added Russell.

"But—how—I don't understand!" Minka exclaimed. Her tail sproinged into the shape of a question mark. "What about all of Blythe's sewing supplies? Where will you make the outfits for the new collection?"

"Don't worry about that," Blythe assured her.

"What do you mean?" asked Minka.

"Usually, I design new fashions, then find the perfect fabric for each one. But this time, I thought I'd try something different," Blythe explained. "I'm going to wait until you've finished the paintings and *then* design the fashion line. That way, every outfit will showcase all your artistic genius, and I won't need my sewing room back until you're finished creating the artwork for the fabrics!"

"I don't even know what to say!" Minka said, bounding back and forth between the easel and the canvases and the drawers full of supplies. "I've never had anything like an art studio before. Working right in the middle of Day Camp has always been good enough for me."

"Maybe that was true when art was your hobby," Zoe said, sounding serious. "But you're going to the big time now, Minka. You've got to take your artwork to a whole new level now that you're going to be a professional artist. Just say those beautiful words! Minka Mark, professional artist."

"Minka Mark, professional...artist?" she repeated, with a note of hesitation in her voice. Minka had never set out to be a professional anything. She made art because she loved it. It was as simple as that.

"Doesn't that sound good?" gushed Zoe.

"I...guess," Minka said doubtfully, but it seemed like nobody noticed.

"Being a professional demands a different mind-set, you know," Russell told Minka. He opened last month's issue of *Animals Abound!* magazine and propped it against the easel's smooth surface. "My owner was going to recycle this magazine, but I thought you might find inspiration in the feature article."

Minka glanced at the headline. "Gaston LeChien!" she exclaimed. "He's my favorite-favorite-*favorite* animal artist of all time!"

"Well, guess what? *Animals Abound!* interviewed Gaston's manager about his artistic process," Russell said. "Anyway, I thought it might be interesting."

"Sounds great, Russell. Thanks!" Minka said. But inside, she wondered, *Artistic process? What do those words even mean?*

"We'd better leave you to create in peace," Penny Ling spoke up.

"I'd never want to disturb an artistic genius at work!" added Pepper—and for once, she wasn't joking around.

"But we'll be right in Day Camp if you need us," Blythe said.

"And I'll be waiting right outside your door!" Zoe promised. "Whatever I can do to help, Minka, just let me know. I mean it! Cleaning brushes, getting snacks, sharpening pencils. No job is too big or too small."

"Thanks, everybody," Minka said gratefully. She knew how hard they'd worked just to create this special space for her, and she appreciated it more than she could say. "Where would I be without you?"

As her friends filed out of Minka's brand-new art studio and closed the door, she realized exactly where she would be without them: completely and totally alone. The stillness of the little room was overwhelming. If Minka listened very carefully, she could faintly hear their voices through the door.

Minka took a deep breath. *Time to get to work, I guess,* she thought. Minka pulled a large blank canvas off the shelf and propped it up against the easel. For a long moment, Minka stared at it. *Now what?* she wondered.

That was weird. Minka had never asked that question before about painting. Normally, when she approached a blank canvas, Minka's creativity surged, and she knew exactly what to do.

Minka reached for a few tubes of bright acrylic paints. Hot pink, pumpkin orange, yellow as bright as a blazing sun. The colors Minka chose were vivid and cheery, the perfect contrast to the gloomy gray weather outside. With a satisfied smile, Minka squirted three round puddles of paint onto her palette. The wet paint glimmered under the studio lights; Minka could already tell that her canvas would be a wild explosion of happy colors. She didn't waste a moment grabbing her favorite paintbrush.

Swoosh! Swish! Splat!

Minka painted fast; that was her favorite way to work, letting the colors lead the way. A streak of pink, a sunburst of orange, a splash of yellow. Minka made sure that her brush was so loaded with paint that some of her strokes left long drips of paint trailing down the canvas, like crazy-colored raindrops. That was how it felt for Minka when she painted. An amazing, swirling storm of colors and ideas surrounded her, sweeping her away like a pleasant, powerful tornado.

Then, like a storm blowing over, Minka was done. Somehow, she always just *knew* when a painting was finished and it was time to put down her brush.

An enormous grin spread across Minka's face as she examined her painting. Amazingly, all the happiness that Minka felt when she was making art had been captured on that canvas. No matter where she hung it, Minka could already tell that her newest painting would brighten up a room.

Then her smile faded. *Wait a second,* she reminded herself. *This isn't supposed to go on a wall. It's supposed to go on people and pets! Didn't Zoe say something about clashing colors and complementary colors and all that stuff? Would people want to wear pink and orange and yellow all at the same time?*

Minka tapped her foot, deep in thought as she pondered the question. Humans seemed to wear a lot of dark colors, she thought…especially the serious business-type people who rushed in and out of the Littlest Pet Shop in the evenings, grabbing a new accessory or fun toy for their pets on their way home from work. Minka couldn't imagine any of them ever wearing a pattern so big…so bright…so *loud*. Her shoulders sagged as she slid the canvas off the easel and carefully propped it against the wall to dry. *It will still be nice to hang on the wall,* she told herself. *And I've got* plenty *of other canvases to paint—Blythe and Zoe made sure of that.*

Minka bounded over to the drawers of art supplies and reached for a tube of sky-blue paint. *With some purple and pink and green…* she began.

Then Minka stopped. *Don't make the same mistake as last time,* she reminded herself as she put the blue paint back and pulled out a tube of navy. One color wasn't enough, so Minka reached for a tube of purple paint that was so dark it almost looked black. Then she started to paint. Stripes, stripes, stripes—wide and thin, short and long. No splatters or splashes this time. Every stroke Minka made was careful and cautious. Even after a tiny voice inside told her to stop, Minka kept painting more and more and even more stripes, until there wasn't a single sliver of blank canvas left. Soon the navy and purple stripes were touching, then overlapping, until they became a single blob of paint, and even the stripes disappeared.

When Minka was finished, her newest painting looked like a dark tunnel without a hint of light—but when it became fabric, would anyone want to *wear* it? Minka wasn't sure, but the longer she stared at it, the more she had to admit that it didn't seem even a little bit unique or special. Those were some of the most important characteristics for the fashion line that Blythe was going to design.

Back to the drawing board, Minka told herself as she scampered across the studio for a new canvas. *Or maybe I should say, back to the painting board!*

On her way to get a new canvas, Minka spotted the copy of *Animals Abound!* that Russell had brought in. *Maybe I should take a look at that article about Gaston LeChien,*

Minka thought. She flipped through the magazine until she found a big photograph of Gaston, looking especially serious with a dark beret perched on his head.

GASTON THE GREAT

by Maritza Ramos

Anyone who knows anything about art knows that French bulldog painter Gaston LeChien is one of the animal art world's brightest stars—and the anticipation for his next show, which will be held right here in the heart of Downtown City, is reaching a fever pitch. But who *is* the pooch behind the paintings?

To find out, I made arrangements for a tour of Gaston's studio, but the notoriously reclusive artist was nowhere to be found. His manager, Juliette Peindre, told me more.

"Gaston works in complete solitude," Ms. Peindre explained. "While he is creating, he sees no one—not even his friends and family. Gaston knows that the smallest distraction could threaten his entire creative process. He's so dedicated to his art that weeks—even months—will pass before he is ready to emerge from the cocoon of his art studio. A master like Gaston lives his philosophy: Art first—and always."

Weeks! Minka thought in shock as her tail formed the shape of a question mark.

Months! She could hardly imagine going even two days without seeing her friends. But if Gaston, one of the greatest artists in the world, had figured out the secret to producing fantastic art, who was Minka to argue?

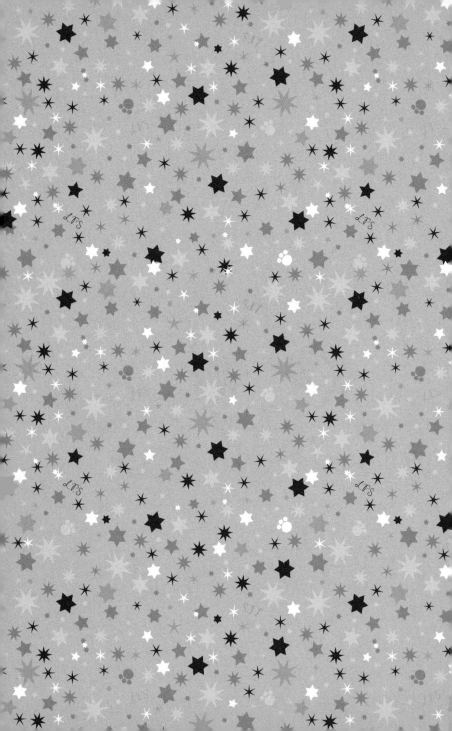

Chapter 4

Outside the art studio, the other pets were trying to enjoy Day Camp like they usually did, but something was missing.

"It's just not the same without Minka," Penny Ling finally spoke up, saying what everyone was thinking.

"I keep expecting to see her at her easel,

splashing paint around," Russell said. "I wish she could do her paintings out here."

"But we wouldn't want to be a distraction," Zoe reminded him. "Minka needs our support more than anything."

"I know," Pepper said. "I just miss her!"

Russell looked thoughtful. "Well, it *is* almost snack time," he said. "Even artists have to eat, right? Maybe Minka can have a snack with us."

Vinnie brightened immediately. "Great idea, Russell!" he exclaimed. "Minka's working so hard that she deserves an extra-special snack. Something that will give her energy to keep at it!"

"Are you thinking what I'm thinking?" Sunil asked Vinnie, who nodded eagerly.

"Leave snack time to us!" Vinnie declared. He and Sunil then zoomed off to the kitchen.

Zoe glanced at the clock on the wall. "It *has* been a few hours. I suppose it wouldn't hurt if we checked in," she said as she beckoned to Russell. "Come on, let's go see if Minka needs anything."

Zoe and Russell crossed the room and knocked on the studio door. At first, there was no answer, but when Zoe knocked again, Minka opened the door just a crack and peeked out with a wild look in her eyes. "What? What is it?" she asked.

"Hey, Minka! How's it going?" asked Zoe.

"Fine. It's fine!" Minka said quickly.

"Do you need any help?" Russell said.

"What? Whoa—wait a minute—who said anything about needing help?" Minka asked, talking even faster than usual. "Everything's fine! I'm doing just fine in here!"

"Great news!" Zoe said. "Can we see?"

"No!" Minka howled, so loud that everyone else jumped.

"I'm sorry," Zoe said. "That was my bad. I forget sometimes that artists don't like to show their work until they're ready."

But Russell's forehead wrinkled in concern. "Are you *sure* everything's okay?" he asked Minka.

Minka tried to laugh, but it didn't sound right. "Of course!" she babbled. "Why wouldn't it be?"

"You just seem a little…anxious," Russell told her.

"Stressed out," Zoe added.

"It's, uh, these paintbrushes," Minka said, waving them in the air and accidentally spraying her pals with splatters of paint. "I need to wash them, but I don't have *time*—"

"I can do it," Zoe offered as she reached for the brushes. "Here—let me help."

"Thanks, Zoe, you're a lifesaver," Minka said gratefully. She started to close the door, but Russell stuck his foot in it just in time.

"Minka, it's snack time," he told her. "Come eat with us."

But Minka shook her head. "Eat? Who has time to eat?" she replied.

Russell and Zoe exchanged a look of concern. "Minka. You have to *eat*," Zoe told her. "Everybody has to eat. Even hardworking artistic geniuses."

Minka glanced over her shoulder. "Guys, I really have to get back to work," she said. "The paint's drying and..."

"Okay, here's a compromise," Russell

suggested. "We'll bring a snack to you, and you can eat it whenever you're ready to take a break."

"Perfect! Thanks! Bye!" Minka said, slamming the door in their faces.

For a moment, Russell and Zoe just stood there, staring at the door.

"That was weird," Russell said. "I mean, *really* weird, and for Minka, that's saying a lot."

"I hope she isn't letting the pressure get to her," Zoe said in a worried voice. "You know Minka can get a little…carried away sometimes."

"To put it lightly," Russell said, looking as concerned as Zoe sounded.

"It's up to us to look out for her," Zoe said. "We've got to make sure that Minka eats and rests and—"

"And has a little fun sometimes," Russell

interrupted. "Nobody can work *all* the time—even if they're doing something they love."

"I don't know," Zoe said. "She seems pretty determined to do nothing but paint, paint, paint. Maybe the studio was a bad idea."

"I don't think it was a bad idea, exactly," Russell told her. "I think Minka just needs a few reminders about balancing work and play. That's all."

"We can definitely help her out there," Zoe replied. "Come on—let's go wash these brushes in the sink before they get all dried out. That kind of stress is the last thing Minka needs!"

Russell followed Zoe to the kitchen, where they found the biggest mess either one of them had ever seen. Three eggs had fallen to the floor and broken, making a slimy, oozing puddle. Clouds of flour drifted through the air like a snowstorm. Four pans sizzled on the stove while the mixer whirled. Worst of all was a pile of banana peels that nearly reached to the ceiling, and right in the middle of it all stood Vinnie and Sunil, wearing white aprons and chef hats!

"Banana muffins, coming right up!" Sunil announced as he lifted the mixer out of a large bowl, but Sunil forgot to turn the mixer off first. When he lifted it out of the bowl, muffin batter sprayed all over the room! Zoe and Russell ducked just in time, but Vinnie, who was standing at the stove, wasn't so lucky. Two giant globs of batter flew right into his eyes!

"Ahhhhhh! I can't see a thing!" he howled. "Sunil! You gotta help me!"

"I can't!" Sunil yelled. "This mixer is not cooperating!"

"But the banana pancakes are burning—I can smell them! Somebody better flip them—fast!" Vinnie pleaded as he frantically wiped his eyes.

"What is going on here?" Zoe shouted, raising her voice so that she could be heard over all the noise. Russell rushed over to turn off Sunil's mixer.

Sunil and Vinnie turned to look at her. For a moment, nobody spoke.

"It's, uh, snack time?" Sunil said at last.

"You call this a snack?" Russell asked in astonishment, gesturing to the plates and platters piled high with food.

Vinnie shrugged. "We didn't know what Minka wanted to eat, so we thought we'd make everything. Banana pancakes—"

"Banana muffins," Sunil added.

"Banana splits!"

"Peanut butter and banana sandwiches!"

"Banana milk shakes!"

"Banana bread!"

"Banana pudding!"

"Banana cream pie!"

"Chocolate-covered bananas on a stick!"

"This isn't a snack," Zoe said. "It's a feast!"

Vinnie stood back and surveyed the mess in the kitchen. "Maybe we went a little...bananas," he admitted.

"Maybe? *Maybe?*" Zoe echoed in disbelief. "I think the word you're looking for is 'definitely.'"

Sunil's shoulders slumped. "Sorry," he said.

"Don't be sorry!" Zoe assured him. "This is exactly what Minka needs from us right now."

"A nine-course, banana-based meal?" Vinnie asked hopefully.

"Friends who are willing to go above and beyond for her," Zoe corrected him. "So you two finish cooking, and Russell and I will start cleaning."

"One step ahead of you, Zoe!" Russell called out as he plucked broken bits of eggshell off the floor. "This gives me an idea, too. What if we ask Pepper and Penny Ling to plan something special for Minka's break time?"

"Something special? Like a mani-pedi and a massage?" asked Zoe.

"Something like that…but designed just for Minka," Russell explained. "Like an obstacle course or a scavenger hunt. Something with big fun and big activity."

"An obstacle course—that would be perfect for Minka!" cried Zoe. She beckoned to Pepper and Penny Ling and told them the whole plan to create something fun to help Minka relax. Cleaning was not exactly Zoe's favorite activity in the world, but she couldn't help smiling as she reached for the mop. With everybody else working so hard to support Minka, Zoe just knew that her new paintings would be destined for greatness!

* *

Back in the studio, Minka leaned against the wall and closed her eyes. It was very quiet in the studio—and very quiet outside, too. Minka couldn't hear any chatter or laughter through the door. *If it stopped raining, they probably all went for a walk*, Minka thought sadly. *I wish I could've gone, too.*

But Minka knew that wasn't possible—not when she hadn't managed to create a single painting that was good enough for Blythe's new collection. The floor of the studio was littered with discarded canvases, painted in almost every color scheme and pattern that Minka could imagine. The more she painted, the less sure Minka felt about what she should do next. Every choice she had to make was an agony. Thick brush? Thin brush? Flat-edged brush? Tapered brush? Minka didn't know which one to choose—and forget about picking out paint. From the different types to the different colors, Minka was practically paralyzed. The last couple canvases had just a few spots of paint on them before Minka gave up.

The only thing Minka was certain about was that she was failing—big time. If she failed, she wouldn't just be hurting an important effort to help the endangered animals. She'd be letting Blythe and her pet friends down, too.

That made Minka feel worse than anything. She wished she could run out of the studio and ask her friends for help, for advice, for anything, really. Minka reached for the doorknob, then stopped herself. *Remember Gaston*, she thought. *Remember how a real artist works: Art first and always.*

Minka took a deep breath and reached for another paintbrush. But before she could choose one, her shoulders slumped in defeat.

I don't know enough about fashion to create fabric, Minka thought. *Zoe and Blythe's crash course proved that. If only there was somewhere I could go to learn more—like a library or a school or—*

"The Fashion District!" Minka gasped. It was so obvious! Why hadn't she thought of this before? Downtown City had a bustling fashion district, filled with glittering showrooms and gleaming runways, professional models and famous designers, and the absolute latest in cutting-edge fashion. There wasn't a better place in the world to get an immediate education in the finer points of fashion, and best of all, it was just a few blocks away.

I can go, watch, listen, and learn—and be back before lunch! Minka thought in excitement. As Minka made a plan, her tail lost its droop and her shoulders lost their slump. She bounded across the floor, opened the door, and poked her head out. There was no sign of her friends in Day Camp, but she could hear a lot of giggling coming from the kitchen. For about half a second, Minka was tempted to see what was so funny.

But she shook her head instead. *Focus on the fashion. Art first and always*, she reminded herself. Besides, it was better that everyone else was busy having so much fun. That way, they wouldn't notice that Minka was gone.

Minka crept through Day Camp and jumped onto a chair, opened the window, and then pulled herself through it. She took a deep breath…

And jumped down to the sidewalk below!

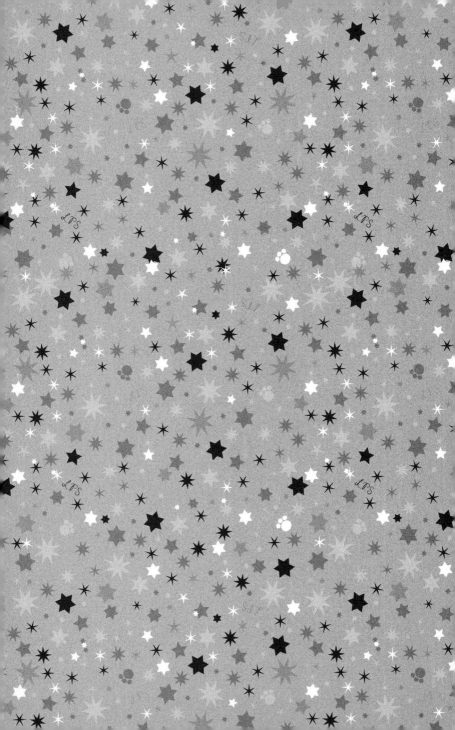

Chapter 5

Minka stood on the sidewalk, blinking her eyes as the sun finally burst through the clouds. She'd never been on her own in Downtown City, and it suddenly seemed bigger, louder, and even more exciting than ever before. There were cars and taxis honking in the streets, bicyclists snaking through the traffic, and plenty of people crowding the sidewalks. Minka ducked behind a trash can just in time to avoid being zoomed over by a boy on a skateboard—where she found a pigeon pecking at a French fry.

"Is it *always* like this?" Minka asked the pigeon, even though she already knew the answer. The pigeon said nothing as it nabbed the fry with its pointy beak and flew off.

Minka took a deep breath. *You can do this*, she told herself. *Art first and always!*

Then, Minka scampered down the sidewalk, making sure to hide behind newspaper stands and streetlights whenever she could. Everybody knew that Downtown City was a place where just about anything could happen, but Minka had a feeling that it wasn't every day that a pink monkey roamed the streets all by herself. She definitely didn't want to attract any attention that might interfere with her mission.

Whenever Minka passed by a bus stop, she paused to check the map posted there to make sure she was still on the right path. *That's what Russell would do*, Minka thought, feeling proud of herself for thinking of such a smart plan. Of course, if Zoe had tagged along on Minka's outing, there would be no need for a map. Zoe could find her way to the Fashion District even if she were blindfolded!

Left turn, straight, look both ways and cross the street, straight, another left turn— and Minka had arrived. Most street signs in Downtown City were bright green, but the ones in the Fashion District were painted deep purple with shimmering gold trim. But even without the signs, Minka would've known exactly where she was. The Fashion District was just as busy and bustling as the rest of Downtown City, but there was something different about it, too. Minka saw people unloading bolts of beautiful fabric from the back of a white van. If she listened carefully near one of the open windows, Minka could hear the clatter of dozens of sewing machines at work. Other people were carting lights into a studio, where the words HOUSE OF D'ADAMO were painted on the window. *I wonder if they're setting up for a fashion show,* Minka thought as she watched a group of models following the light crew. Behind them, two assistants pushed a large cart filled with props and accessories, including an enormous hat with a frothy veil. The hat was so big that Minka could've used it for a bed.

And that gave her an idea.

While the assistants waited for the light to change so they could cross the street, Minka crept toward the cart. She watched them carefully, waiting for the perfect moment when they would both be distracted enough that Minka could sneak onto the cart. Minka knew she would have to act fast, though. If the light changed and the assistants crossed the street, Minka might not get another opportunity to sneak into the fashion studio.

Minka was in luck! A man on a motorcycle swerved and hit a trash can, making a tremendous *boom* as the metal can rattled down the street, spilling garbage everywhere! Residents of Downtown City were used to plenty of noise in the heart of the city—but this still got their attention.

"Did you see that?" one of the assistants asked, wrinkling her nose.

"Gross!" added the other.

Minka didn't care how disgusting the trash mess was. She knew that this was her chance. She was a blur of pink fur as she clambered up the cart, flicked over the hat, and tucked herself under its crown. Minka moved so fast that no one noticed her—not even the assistants standing on either side of the cart.

"Come on, let's get this stuff across the street," Minka heard one of the assistants say, though the sound of her voice was muffled through the fuzzy felt hat. "I don't know if you've worked with Diane D'Adamo before, but she's *intense*. We do *not* want to be late."

Bump! Bump! Thump!

The metal cart rattled over the pavement, making Minka's teeth chatter. She wished she could've held on to something, but there were no handles under the hat. All Minka could do was hope that the hat wouldn't fall off the cart!

Minka shifted suddenly as the cart took a sharp turn. Peeking through the veil, Minka could see that the cart was moving into the fashion studio. *Yes!* Minka thought in a silent cheer. She could hardly believe that her plan was working so well!

Minka crossed her fingers while she waited to find out where the cart would end up. She was even more amazed when the assistants wheeled the cart right in front of the catwalk!

"We've got the accessories," one of the assistants said breathlessly.

"Fabulous," a new voice replied as she clapped her hands twice. "Okay, everyone, let's get this fitting started!"

I bet that's Diane D'Adamo, Minka thought. She didn't know much about fashion, but the name was so familiar that Minka was pretty sure she'd heard Blythe or Zoe mention it before. It took all of Minka's focus to sit very still, not moving a muscle, when all she wanted was to jump around for joy. Who would've thought that Minka could manage to get front-row seats at a fashion fitting featuring the clothing of a famous designer? *This is beyond great,* Minka thought in excitement. *It's going to be perfect!*

Minka peered through the tiny holes of the veil to watch what happened next. Each model was wearing a different dress—some long, some short, some fancy with oodles of beads and bangles, some simple without even a single button. The dresses couldn't have been more different, but they had one big thing in common: They all looked amazing! Even Minka, who was no fashion expert, could tell how splendid they were. But how?

It's the fabric, Minka thought all of a sudden. Each dress was made of the perfect fabric for the style. When the fabric and the design were put together, they made each other better. They went together like a peanut butter and banana sandwich.

"I want to see some hats!" Diane D'Adamo called out, but Minka was barely paying attention as she observed the beautiful clothes on display.

It starts with me, Minka realized. *When my paintings are finished and fabric is made from*

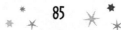

them, Blythe will know just which designs will work best. All I have to do . . . is paint them.

But that was easier said than done. Just thinking about going back into the tiny art studio, all by herself, made Minka feel so anxious that she couldn't help it . . . her tail twitched, once, then twice, then three times in a row!

"Did something on the cart move?" one of the assistants asked.

Minka froze.

"No, of course not," the other assistant replied. "How could hats and scarves move by themselves?"

"I don't know," the assistant replied. "But I really thought I saw something move. Do you think there could be a rat on the cart? I *hate* rats, but you know they're everywhere in a—"

A loud clap interrupted her. "I *asked* for hats!" Diane D'Adamo said, louder this time.

Oh no! Minka thought in a wild panic. If they tried to take *her* hat—the one that had seemed like the perfect hiding place—

"Sorry!" the assistants said at the same time as they scrambled toward the cart.

Not mine—not mine—not mine—not mine, Minka thought again and again. She sat on her tail to keep it from twitching.

"The green one?" one of the assistants asked.

"No. Too simple. We need something *dramatic* to complete this ensemble," Diane D'Adamo said.

Through the veil, Minka saw the other assistant pick up a blue hat with peacock feathers and purple rhinestones. "How about this one?" she asked.

"*Way* too much," Diane D'Adamo replied. "It needs to be attention-grabbing without distracting from the dress. You know, understated. Elegant. How about the big one there—with the veil?"

Minka saw a pair of hands reaching for her hat. A sudden bright light made Minka blink as her hat was lifted into the air, but besides that, she didn't move a muscle. *Maybe my luck will continue and they won't even notice me,* Minka thought, sitting as still as a statue.

Unfortunately, it didn't.

"What's that?" Diane D'Adamo asked. "It looks like a...pink monkey?"

"I'm so sorry! It probably belongs on the prop cart," one of the assistants said. "I have no idea how it got here."

They think I'm, like, a decoration or something,

Minka thought in amazement. Maybe every-thing was going to turn out okay after all.

"I don't care where it goes—just get it off my accessory cart," Diane D'Adamo said, sounding annoyed. "Kayla! Try on the hat and let's see how it looks."

While one of the assistants brought the hat over to a model, the other reached for Minka.

She's going to pick me up, Minka thought. *Not under the arms—not under the arms—*

Naturally, the assistant grabbed Minka right under her arms.

Minka couldn't help it. She was too ticklish. She dissolved into giggles, twitching and shak-ing as she threw back her head in laughter.

Everything happened very fast after that.

The assistant dropped Minka back on the cart and yelped. "It's alive!"

Across the room, the other assistant screamed, "What is it? A rat? Is it a rat?"

Minka pulled herself up to her full height and yelled, "I'm no rat!" But all the people in the studio heard was outraged chattering.

The models screamed in terror and began to run in all directions. One of them accidentally rammed into the cart, which zoomed across the room. Hats and scarves and sparkly pieces of jewelry flew everywhere as Minka held on tight for the ride of her life!

Oh no, Minka thought as the cart picked up speed. *We're going to hit the wall!*

Just in the nick of time, Minka leaped off the cart—and crashed into the makeup table! Clouds of powder and perfume filled the air, making Minka cough and choke.

When the air cleared, Minka realized just what a mess she'd made.

In the panicked stampede, two models had twisted their ankles. Three had torn their dresses. One had lost her shoe. The floor was littered with accessories, from broken jewelry to crushed hats to ripped scarves. The fashion studio was a complete and total disaster!

Diane D'Adamo stood up, looked at the chaos around her, and gritted her teeth. "Get—me—that—rat," she growled.

There was only one thing Minka could do. *Run!*

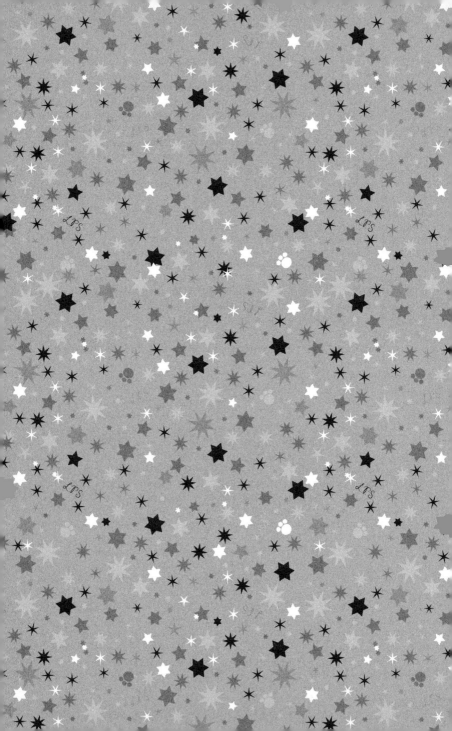

Chapter 6

Back at Day Camp, the pets had never been more proud. Everything was ready for Minka's break time! Sunil and Vinnie had outdone themselves in the kitchen—with a little help from Blythe, of course. As soon as all the yummy food was ready, Russell and Zoe had set up a pretty table right outside Minka's studio and piled it high with the banana treats.

"Look at all this food!" Blythe marveled. "And it smells delicious!"

"The only problem Minka will have is figuring out what to eat first," Russell said.

"We can help her with that," Vinnie spoke up as he stuck one of his long, sticky toes into the whipped cream on top of the banana split.

"Vinnie!" Zoe exclaimed. "How *dare* you? That's for Minka!"

"Sorry," Vinnie mumbled.

Blythe rested her hand on Zoe's head. "It's okay, Zoe. There's plenty more in the kitchen," she said gently.

"Good! Once we get through with her, Minka will have worked up an *enormous* appetite!" Pepper said. She and Penny Ling had spent the morning building a fun obstacle course out of foam blocks, tubes, Hula-Hoops, and jump ropes. It was the perfect place for an energetic monkey to romp and explore.

"Zoe, why don't you go ahead and let Minka know that her snack is ready," Blythe suggested.

Zoe looked worried. "I don't know," she began. "What if we interrupt her right in the middle of a moment of pure genius? I would feel absolutely *horrible* if I interfered with her artistic inspiration!"

"I don't think Minka would mind," Blythe said. "She's pretty used to interruptions from painting out here in Day Camp."

"Yeah, that's true!" Vinnie spoke up. "Pretty much anytime somebody's doing something fun, Minka takes a break to join in."

"It's never hurt her paintings before," Penny Ling added, gesturing to all of Minka's cheerful canvases hanging on the walls.

"You're all right, of course," Zoe admitted. She tiptoed over to the studio's door and tapped quietly.

There was no answer.

"Oh well. Guess she's so busy working that she doesn't want to be interrupted," Zoe said.

Blythe frowned a little. "Or maybe she didn't hear you," she said as she crossed the room. "After all, Minka knows that we were making her a snack."

Blythe knocked on the door and called out, "Minka? Ready for a break?"

Everyone waited expectantly, but still there was no response.

"Maybe Minka *is* so busy working she

doesn't want to stop," Blythe said with a shrug as she moved away from the door. "But I'm sure she'll be out soon. After all, she did say she was hungry."

"And speaking of hungry…" Vinnie said, rubbing his stomach.

Blythe laughed. "Yes, let's all go ahead and eat now," she told him. "I'm sure Minka won't mind."

"Maybe she's almost finished. Then we can all spend the rest of the day having fun!" Pepper said excitedly.

"Maybe she is," Blythe agreed. "Now— last one to the kitchen is a rotten banana!"

*
* *

A few hours later, Minka's banana split had melted into a gooey puddle, but she still hadn't emerged from her studio—and everyone was starting to worry. Even Vinnie and Sunil lost interest in their game of checkers as they waited for Minka to come out.

"You know what? I don't care if she's painting the most amazing artwork the world has ever seen," Russell finally said. "Minka still has to *eat*."

"Yes, I completely agree," Zoe said. "This has gone on for too long."

"Russell, would you knock on Minka's door again?" asked Blythe. "And knock *loudly*."

Russell balled up his paw into a tight little fist and banged on the door. "Minka!" he hollered. "Come out already!"

The others clustered around the door, anxiously waiting for Minka to appear. The minutes ticked by slowly, until Vinnie suddenly said, "Let's knock it down, everybody!"

"Guys—wait—" Blythe began.

But it was too late. Vinnie, Sunil, and Russell were already catapulting toward the door at top speed! They kicked it with all their strength.

Bang!

The door opened so hard and so fast that it hit the wall. With just one look, everyone realized that the art studio was empty.

Minka was gone.

"What happened here?" Russell asked in astonishment. When they had left the studio that morning, it was neat and tidy. It was now a complete mess. Discarded canvases were scattered everywhere. Tubes of paint had been left without their caps on.

A glass of water was crammed with used paintbrushes waiting to be cleaned. It was so messy and cluttered that it would've been impossible for anyone to paint in it.

"Look," Penny Ling said in a soft voice as she held up a canvas with a big blue frowning face on it. "Poor Minka. I guess things weren't going very well in here."

"But why didn't she *tell* us?" Zoe asked. "I don't understand why she didn't say anything!"

"Maybe she didn't know how," Blythe suggested. "Maybe she was embarrassed. It can be really, really hard when you're not getting that creative spark."

"But that's exactly what friends are for!" Zoe said. "We would've helped her—"

"And we still will," Blythe promised. "But first, we have to figure out where she went."

"How do you know for sure that she left?" asked Penny Ling. "Maybe she's hiding here in Day Camp—or somewhere in the store—"

"I guess that's possible," Russell said. "After all, we've been hanging out all day. I can't imagine how she could've slipped past us without anybody noticing."

"Okay, first things first, we're going to search Day Camp and the Littlest Pet Shop," Blythe announced. "Leave no pillow unturned, no cubby unchecked. Operation Find That Monkey starts *now*!"

There was a tremendous commotion in Day Camp as Blythe and all the pets began their search, looking high and low for Minka, calling her name. Pepper and Penny Ling were just about to dismantle their obstacle course when Vinnie suddenly started yelling.

"Come here, everybody! You've gotta see this!" he shouted as he stared at the TV, where the afternoon news had just started.

All eyes turned toward the screen, where the words "Couture Catastrophe!" were flashing.

"Uh-oh," Blythe said.

"In the heart of Downtown City's Fashion District, preparations for designer Diane D'Adamo's upcoming show turned into a downright disaster today when an apparent rodent invasion caused chaos on the catwalk," the newscaster began. "Reports from the scene are conflicting, but at least two sources have confirmed that a strange, pink-hued, long-tailed creature ran amok in the showroom not long ago. We'll bring you more information about this breaking story as we receive it, and now a traffic update from—"

Blythe reached for the remote and turned off the TV. Her mouth was set in a thin, worried line. "Well, I guess we know where Minka is," she began.

"Now let's go get her!" Zoe finished.

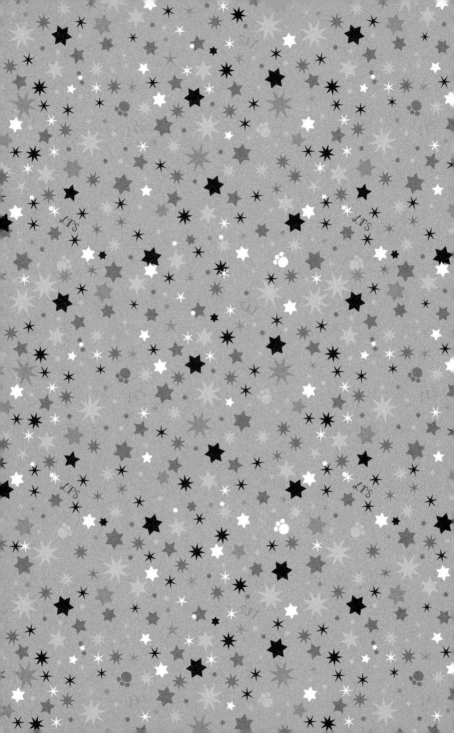

Chapter 7

Meanwhile, Minka darted and dashed through Diane D'Adamo's studio as the assistants chased after her. She didn't know exactly where she was going. All she knew was that she had to get away—fast! She was not about to get caught by a pair of assistants who thought she was a rat.

Past the models, past the bolts of fabric, past the lights, past the makeup, through the hallway, until at last Minka saw the big glass doors directly in front of her. *I'm almost out of here!* she thought in exhilaration, pushing forward with an extra burst of speed.

There was just one problem: Would she be able to open the heavy glass door all by herself?

Minka wasn't sure—but she was about to find out. Not only was she fast approaching the doors, she could hear someone behind her yelling, "It went that way! Hurry! Catch it!"

I'm not *an it!* Minka thought indignantly. She didn't have time to get too offended, though—not when freedom was so close. The glass doors were just inches away!

Minka braced herself for impact, hoping that she would be strong enough to push the door open. But before she hit the glass—

Whoosh!

All of a sudden, Minka found herself flying through the air—right onto the streets of Downtown City!

"Whoa-a-a-ahhhhhhh!" Minka howled as she sailed over the sidewalk. She glanced over her shoulder and spotted a delivery guy disappearing into the House of D'Adamo. Somehow, he'd arrived just in time to pull the door open for Minka!

"I'm freeeeeee!" she squealed in excitement, but Minka knew it was too soon to celebrate. The last thing the little monkey wanted to do was crash-land in the middle of the street and rushing traffic.

The streetlight, Minka thought suddenly. If she could somehow reach out and grab hold of it as she zoomed overhead, she could easily climb down to the ground. But if she missed—if she made a mistake and overshot—Minka knew that she might fall into the street instead.

She *definitely* didn't want that to happen.

"Here we go," Minka told herself. "One—two—*threeeeeeeeeee!*"

Minka stretched her arms as far as they would go—then her fingers—she stretched and she reached and she grasped and, suddenly, there it was: the cool, hard metal, clutched tightly between her hands.

Minka was so relieved she started to laugh and she slid down the pole, just like a firefighter. "Wheeeee!" she cried in delight.

At last, her back feet touched the pavement. Minka darted down the sidewalk, as far from the House of D'Adamo as possible. Finally, when she was absolutely, positively, 100 percent certain that she wasn't being followed, Minka paused to catch her breath. She leaned against a sturdy brick wall and wondered, *What am I going to do now?*

As much as Minka wished it were otherwise, her outing to the Fashion District hadn't been as helpful as she had hoped. She still wasn't entirely sure how to tackle the biggest project of her life—especially when so much was riding on it.

If I go back to the Littlest Pet Shop now, I might let everybody down, Minka thought sadly as she stared at the gum-speckled sidewalk under her feet.

But where else could she go? Downtown City was very big, and Minka was pretty small.

She *definitely* didn't want to be out here, all by herself, when night fell. How would she get dinner? Where would she sleep? No, at some point, she'd have to go home again, whether she was ready to or not.

"I just wish—" Minka began. Then she looked up, and her eyes got so wide they almost popped out of her head.

Right across the street, a glittering gold sign read GASTON LECHIEN: ART FROM THE HEART. OPENING TONIGHT!

"It's not possible," Minka said as she rubbed her eyes with her little hands. "I'm just imagining it…"

But when Minka opened her eyes again, the sign was still there. She'd run wildly through the streets of Downtown City and ended up right in front of the art gallery featuring her favorite artist's new paintings!

Minka walked across the street as if she were in a dream and pressed her face against the art gallery's front window. Maybe if she could see some of Gaston's paintings—if she could just catch a glimpse of them—she would find the inspiration she needed to make her own artwork again.

Sadly, there were large white screens covering each window to keep the paintings secret before the big unveiling. Minka sighed as she leaned against the window, and then slid all the way down to the ground. She should've figured there would be screens. It was what she would do if she were going to have a big art show for her paintings—a dream that seemed further away than ever.

Just then, a shadow passed over Minka.

"What is this?" a voice asked in an elegant

French accent. "Why, I have never seen such a sad little monkey before in all my life!"

Minka glanced up—directly into the face of Gaston himself! With his glossy golden fur, dark muzzle, and jaunty beret, Minka would have recognized him any-where . . . even though she'd never imagined in a million years that she would see him face-to-face!

"But—you—you're—" she spluttered. *"You're Gaston!"*

The famous French bulldog chuckled. "Yes, it is true," he admitted. "And who are you, melancholy monkey in front of my gallery?"

Minka scrambled to her feet, momentarily forgetting all her worries. "I'm your number one fan!" she exclaimed. "I mean, I'm Minka. You can call me Minka."

Gaston laughed again as he held out his paw. "Well, it would be the height of rudeness if I left my number one fan languishing on the sidewalk," he said, his black eyes twinkling. "Would you like a sneak peek of my new show? It's not *quite* ready—I have a few last adjustments to make, some finishing touches—"

"Of course I would!" Minka shrieked with excitement. "Wow! I can't believe this is happening!"

Gaston brought Minka around to the side of the gallery, where a special doggy door had been installed. "I like to call this my private entrance," he said as he held the flap open for Minka. Luckily, she was small enough that she could squeeze through without any trouble.

For a moment, Minka was struck speechless. The art gallery was gorgeous in its simplicity. It had clean white walls, bright, beaming spotlights overhead, and hardwood floors that were as shiny as the surface of a lake on a clear day.

"Please, make yourself at home," Gaston told Minka. "There is a buffet over there. Help yourself! I hope you like the paintings. I will be about—here and there—if you need anything."

Minka found her voice. "Thank you. Thank you, thank you, thank you!" she said.

As Gaston hurried off in one direction, Minka stepped toward the closest painting. It was a large, narrow canvas with a single blue blotch right in the middle of it. Thin gray streaks of paint, so faint that Minka could barely see them, trailed away in all directions. A little card under the painting read RAINBURST, ACRYLIC ON CANVAS.

So cool, Minka marveled. The design was super simple—a sunburst done in the colors of a rainstorm—but powerful at the same time. It was exactly the kind of art that Minka wished she could create.

The next painting was very different. The canvas was almost entirely black, except for a single red dog bowl in the lower left corner. This one's card read EMPTY/ALONE, OIL ON CANVAS.

Gaston really is a genius, Minka thought as she stood back to take in the entire painting. *That's exactly how it feels.*

"How what feels?" Gaston asked, appearing suddenly by Minka's side.

Minka jumped. "Did I say that aloud?" she asked.

"You must have, because I heard you," replied Gaston.

"I love your paintings," Minka told him. "They really... It's hard to describe. They speak to the heart, you know?"

"Thank you!" Gaston said with a modest smile. "That is the hope of every artist, you know. To reach another through his art."

Just then, a pack of puppies came cavorting toward them, yipping and yapping.

"Ah, ah, ah! Be careful, *mes chers chiens*!" Gaston called after them. He turned to Minka. "My nieces and nephews," he explained. "I am very lucky. My entire family travels with me, wherever I go."

"Uncle Gaston! Papa says you need to

add some light to this one," one of the puppies said.

Gaston raised an eyebrow. "Oh, he thinks
so?" he asked.

Another puppy trotted up with a paintbrush held tightly in his mouth. It already
had a blob of white paint on the tip.

Gaston chuckled and shrugged at Minka.
"Big brothers. What can you do?" he said.
"They think they know everything—and
they're usually right!"

Then, Gaston took the paintbrush and
approached the canvas. With a few deft
touches, he added some white highlights to
the bowl. "How does that look?" he asked.

Minka tilted her head. The painting was
hardly changed at all, and yet it looked transformed. Those few white highlights made

the painting more interesting and complex. "It's the *suggestion* of light," Minka said suddenly. "You didn't have to add a lamp or a sun or anything like that. The reflection on the bowl lets us know that there's light nearby, even if we can't see it. And it makes the painting feel...hopeful, I think."

"Yes!" Gaston cried happily. "That's exactly what I was attempting. I am very glad you could see it. Otherwise—well, you know what they say. Try, try, try again, *non*?"

"But—you're a master," Minka said. "The best animal artist in the world."

Gaston waved his paw in the air dismissively. "Those are just words," he said. "I make the same mistakes and missteps as anyone."

Minka still couldn't believe it. "I used to love painting," she said in a quiet voice. "But...I've been trying to do something new…and…well, it has just been a disaster. Everything I try is awful."

"Good!" Gaston said brightly. "That's excellent!"

Minka's face crinkled up. Had she heard him correctly? Before she could respond, Gaston continued.

"If you never fail, you are not taking any risks," he explained. "An artist must always be willing to take risks, to try new things. That is how we challenge ourselves. That is how we improve our skills."

While Minka pondered that, Gaston returned the paintbrush to his nephew. "Run along and tell your papa he was right—as usual," Gaston told the little pup. The whole litter took off together, making such a racket that everyone in the gallery had to laugh.

Gaston smiled proudly at his family. "I don't know where I would be without them," he told Minka.

Now Minka was even more confused. "But…I thought you did all your work alone!" she said. "I read in *Animals Abound!* that you have to be completely alone when you paint. No interruptions, no distractions…nobody…no puppy."

Gaston shook his head. "That couldn't be further from the truth," he confided in Minka.

"Are you kidding?" she exclaimed. "But I read—"

"That's just a silly story that my manager made up," Gaston explained. "She thought we would sell more paintings if they were—how did she say it? Ah, yes, 'veiled in mystery.' You know, Gaston the 'tortured genius,' committed to his art at the expense of everything else. 'Art first and always,' she says. What nonsense!"

"But—" Minka began.

"The truth is that I don't think I could paint a single stroke if I were apart from them too long," Gaston continued. "My motto is 'Art from the heart.' And that's what my friends and family are—my heart."

"This—this changes *everything*!" Minka exclaimed, so excited that she started to bounce around. "Thank you, thank you, *thank you*!"

Gaston started to laugh. "For what? I didn't—"

"I know what to do now," Minka said in a rush. "Art from the heart. *Friends* first and always. *Of course.*"

Minka stopped bounding around long enough to give Gaston a hug. "Good luck with your show," she told him. "You really are as brilliant as everyone says you are!"

"You can't stay?" asked Gaston.

Minka shook her head. "Not this time," she said. "There's a blank canvas out there just waiting for me!"

"But of course," Gaston said with a look of understanding in his eyes. "I know that feeling. *Bonne chance*, Minka. Perhaps some-day I will see you at your own show!"

Minka was already halfway to the secret doggy door when she paused to take one last look at Gaston and the beautiful art gallery showing his paintings. "Maybe you will!" she called back.

Then she dashed through the doggy door, ready to try, try, try again.

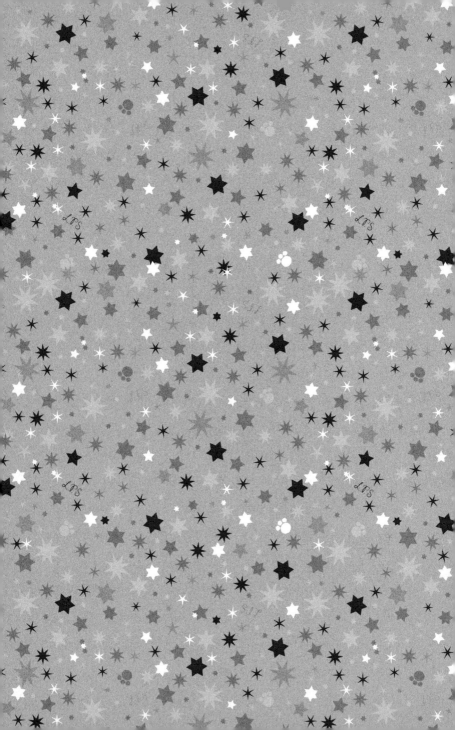

Chapter 8

Minka barreled onto the sidewalk, not caring for a minute if anyone stopped to stare as she zigged and zagged down the street. Minka didn't have time to slink around anymore, trying to avoid attention. She needed to get back to Day Camp immediately! Her fingers were so eager to grab a paintbrush that they were practically twitching. Minka still wasn't entirely sure what she would paint, but that didn't matter anymore. She knew that the inspiration would come; it always did. Minka had to trust the paint and the canvas—and herself. Somehow, she'd stopped doing that, and everything else had unraveled, too. If Minka had reached out to her friends when everything started to fall apart, she knew that they would've helped her.

Now that she knew what needed to be done, Minka felt unstoppable. If only she had wings like the pigeons cooing on the curb, Minka would have flown all the way back to Day Camp. *Wouldn't everybody be surprised if I could do that?* Minka thought, giggling to herself. She'd soar right through the window she'd left open earlier, and everybody would be so shocked, especially Russell, they'd probably all yell out—

"Minka!"

Did someone call my name? Minka wondered, or was her imagination working overtime? She shook her head. It was probably just a coincidence. What were the odds that someone on these crowded sidewalks had recognized her?

But when the call came again, there was no mistaking it: Someone was definitely shouting Minka's name!

Minka was so surprised that she skidded to a stop. *Who's that?* she wondered, whipping her head around. To her utter amazement, all her friends were there—right there!—standing across the street, waving wildly at her.

"Blythe? Zoe? Russell?" Minka gasped. "How did—what are—wait a second—"

Just then, the light changed, and Blythe led the pets across the street to Minka. There was such a jumble of hugs and laughter and happy shouts, that Minka didn't stop bounding from one friend to the next until she'd hugged everybody at least three times.

At last, Minka paused to catch her breath. "How did you find me?" she asked.

Blythe pointed down the street, where several news vans were double-parked. "Did you happen to pay a visit to the House of D'Adamo?" she asked in a serious-sounding voice, but Minka could tell from the way Blythe's eyes were twinkling that she wasn't upset.

"Uh-oh," Minka said with a guilty grin. "Is everything okay over there?"

"It will be," Blythe told her. "There's just one problem—none of the models will go back inside until somebody catches the, uh, 'pink rat' that was 'terrorizing' them!"

"I wasn't terrorizing them!" Minka protested. "I was just looking for some... inspiration. It's not *my* fault that they can't tell a monkey from a rat."

"My guess is that in all the commotion, their eyes played tricks on them," Russell said knowingly. "It happens in high-stress situations."

"And speaking of high-stress situations..." Penny Ling began.

Zoe stepped forward. "We saw your art studio," she said, placing her paw on Minka's hand. "Why didn't you *tell* us you were having trouble?"

Minka shrugged and looked at the ground.

"I was so embarrassed," she admitted. "You'd all worked so hard to fix up that amazing art studio for me…and trusted me with such a great, big, giant, *huge* responsibility…I didn't know how to tell you that I couldn't handle it. That the whole collection might be a giant disaster because of *me*. I didn't want to let you down."

Blythe leaned over to give Minka another hug. "Minka, we're your friends," she said. "You could never let us down even if you tried."

"Maybe I would've realized that if I hadn't insisted on spending every single minute alone in the studio," Minka said ruefully. "I got lonely, and scared, and everything just spiraled out of control."

"Is that why you snuck out the window?" asked Vinnie.

Minka nodded. "I was *desperate*," she explained. "I thought, well, maybe if I took a field trip to the Fashion District…"

"Did it help?" asked Pepper.

"A little," Minka said. "But not how I expected. I'll tell you all about it when—"

"Uh-oh!" Sunil said, pointing down the street.

Everyone turned to look and saw a reporter running toward them.

Minka had been spotted!

"We've got to get out of here—*now*!" Zoe exclaimed.

Blythe and the pets formed a tight circle around Minka, shielding her from view. Then they began running down the street as fast as they could, hoping to escape from the determined reporter and the cameraman trailing behind her. Dodging pedestrians, careening around corners, zipping past parked cars—the streets of Downtown City were like a giant obstacle course! Minka and her pals were having so much fun that they soon forgot all about the chase.

"Hold up!" Blythe yelled, and everyone stopped so suddenly that they piled up in a heap.

"What is it, Blythe?" Zoe asked breathlessly. "Are we lost?"

Blythe shook her head. "No, not lost," she replied, pointing at the colorful awning of the Littlest Pet Shop overhead. "We're back!"

A tiny bell rang as Blythe opened the door for all the pets. Minka paused, for just a moment, before she stepped into the store.

"I'm back," she whispered as a big grin stretched across her face.

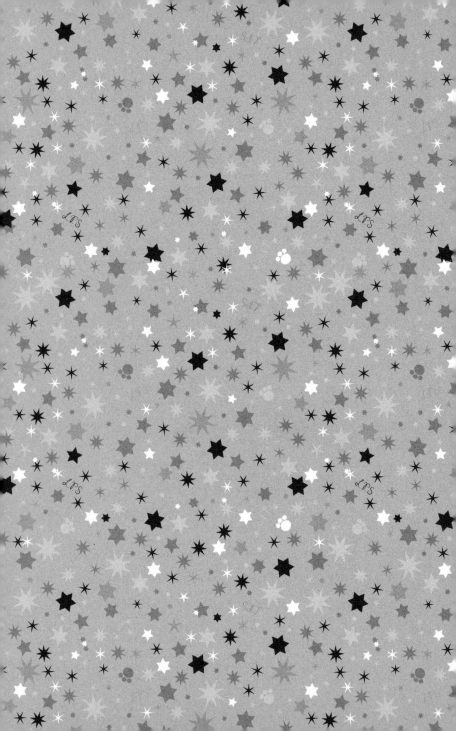

Chapter 9

Minka was a blur as she raced into Day Camp, which had changed while she was gone. For starters, there was a mountain of food stacked up outside the studio door, and even though the ice cream was melted and the sandwiches were soggy, the smell of bananas made Minka's mouth water. She also noticed a fantastic obstacle course that her friends had built in the center of the room. Minka paused and turned around to see everyone gathered behind her.

"Is this for—" Minka began.

All her friends nodded at the same time.

"You guys are the best," Minka told them. "Really and truly!"

"We have lots more food in the kitchen," Vinnie spoke up.

"If you want another banana split, just say the word," Sunil said, snapping his fingers. "I will make you one in no time!"

"Pepper and I built the obstacle course," Penny Ling added. "We thought it would be a fun way to take a break."

"Even artists need breaks after all," Pepper said with a wink.

"That's the truth!" Minka said. "But right now, I think I'm ready to . . ."

Minka's voice trailed off as she dashed into the art studio. The others waited expectantly for her to finish her sentence, but all they heard was the *scraaaatch-scraaaatch-scraaaaape* of something heavy being dragged across the floor.

"Should we help her?" Zoe asked anxiously.

But Blythe shook her head. "I think Minka would let us know if she needed anything," she said. "She's got this!"

Moments later, Minka appeared, dragging the easel behind her. There was a large blank canvas propped on it.

"I need three brushes," Minka said breathlessly. "And green paint—all the green paint!—and some brown and yellow, too."

"We're on it!" Zoe cried as she and Russell hurried into the art studio.

Minka turned to the others. "I had this

 137

crazy idea," she began. "I'm not sure if it will work or not—but—it just might—"

"What's your idea?" asked Vinnie.

But before Minka could answer, Zoe and Russell returned with her supplies. Minka's attention switched to the canvas, completely and utterly focused on one thing only: her artwork.

"This is so exciting," Penny Ling whispered to Zoe. "What do you think she's going to paint?"

"I have no idea," Zoe replied. "But I can't wait to find out!"

Everyone watched, breathless with anticipation, as Minka went to work. *Swish. Swish. Swoosh.* Long strokes of paint in different shades of green filled the canvas from top to bottom, forming vertical lines with just the smallest amount of overlap. Then

Minka used the yellow paint to add shafts of sunlight spilling around the lines. The brown paint became shadows and textures. An hour passed so quickly that it felt like just minutes.

When everyone least expected it, Minka suddenly dropped her paintbrush. "Done!" she announced. "What do you think?"

The room was quiet as the others viewed Minka's painting.

Zoe was the first to speak. "I love it," she announced. "Stripes are so in right now!"

"I can definitely come up with some designs to showcase them," Blythe added. "It has an airy feeling, doesn't it? Light, almost…breezy…"

"It's a bamboo grove!" Penny Ling exclaimed all of a sudden.

All eyes turned to her.

"It is, isn't it?" Penny Ling continued. "I'd recognize it anywhere."

"You're exactly right!" Minka replied. "My idea—well—one of the things endangered animals need most of all is their homes, right? They have special places in the world where they live, and if their homes aren't protected, then they'll be in big trouble. Which is why—"

Suddenly, Minka dashed off to the art studio. She returned with an armload of paint and paintbrushes and a new canvas. Blythe and Zoe exchanged a smile as Minka went back to work. There was no doubt about it now: Minka was *back*!

Minka's next painting featured a swirling pattern in several shades of blue, with a twisting pinkish-orange design that really popped against the cool, watery background.

"A coral reef!" Blythe cried. "Oh, Minka, I love it. This is the *perfect* theme for our new collection! We can call it…Habitats."

"Clothes for where—and how—you live," added Zoe. "I love how when you first look at it, you see a beautiful or interesting pattern, but when you look closer…"

"You realize that it's really the habitat of an endangered animal!" Russell finished for her.

"Minka, you are an absolute genius," Blythe declared.

The compliment made Minka blush even pinker. "Oh, whatever," she said as Vinnie and Sunil brought her a fresh canvas. "You haven't seen anything yet!"

For the rest of the afternoon, Minka painted with a little help from all her friends, who cleaned her brushes, brought her new canvases, and delivered snacks and drinks. No one knew when Minka would be finished, not even Minka herself. She was far too caught up in her art—and the moment—to think ahead like that. For Minka, with a paintbrush in her hand, painting was excitement. It was energy. It was an expression of joy and fun and the freedom to create anything she could dream of. And those were the reasons why Minka had been drawn to painting in the first place.

At last, Minka laid down her paintbrush. "I think that's it," she announced, feeling satisfied and tired at the same time.

Six canvases were propped against the wall. In addition to the bamboo grove and the coral reef, Minka had painted a rain forest bursting with tropical, jewel-toned flowers, a shimmery arctic snowscape filled with swirls of white, gray, and silver sparkles, a desert flecked with gold sand, and a glimmering pink-and-purple sunset sky reflected in a lily-studded pond.

"Oh, Minka!" Blythe exclaimed in delight. "You've outdone yourself!"

The other pets crowded around, oohing and aahing over every painting. Minka was beside herself with happiness—not because she'd finished the paintings, but because she was surrounded by her friends.

"When do you think they'll be dry, Minka?" Russell asked. "I want to make sure we have everything we need to pack them up and ship them to the fabric manufacturer."

"Twenty-four hours, probably," Minka replied.

Blythe grabbed her sketchbook. "That will be more than enough time for me to sketch some designs for our new Habitats collection," she said.

A look of panic suddenly crossed Minka's face. "Blythe—your sewing room!" she began. "I *might* have made a, well, gigantic mess in there, but I promise I'll clean it up right away so you can have your sewing room back."

"No rush," Blythe told her as she pulled up a chair. "I think I'd rather work out here, with all of you!"

"Work, work, work," Zoe said with a sigh. "Shouldn't we celebrate a little first?"

The thought gave Minka a fresh burst of energy. "That's a great idea, Zoe!" she exclaimed. "Be right back!"

"What's Minka planning now?" wondered Pepper.

"A party?" guessed Penny Ling.

"A movie marathon?" Russell asked.

"Banana splits for everyone?" Sunil suggested hopefully.

Minka was laughing as she returned to the easel with one last canvas. "We should do *all* those things," she told her friends. "And while we do them, I'm going to paint us doing them!"

Pepper scrunched up her face. "You're going to celebrate painting...with more painting?" she asked.

Minka nodded. "It *is* my favorite thing to do," she said. "And painting my friends? That would be the best artwork of all! My greatest masterpiece!"